For Eunice, who loves dogs!
With love and thanks G.S.

To perfect pets everywhere,
with love C.J.

tiger tales
5 River Road, Suite 128, Wilton, CT 06897
Published in the United States 2014
Originally published in Great Britain 2013
by Hodder Children's Books
a division of Hachette Children's Books
Text copyright © 2013 Gillian Shields
Illustrations copyright © 2013 Cally Johnson-Isaacs
ISBN-13: 978-1-58925-137-3
ISBN-10: 1-58925-137-7
WKT 0612
Printed in China

For more insight and activities,
visit us at www.tigertalesbooks.com

THAT DOG!

by Gillian Shields

Illustrated by Cally Johnson-Isaacs

The mean, miserable Jones family never took any notice of their dog, even though he was just bursting to be loved.

"That dog is so lazy," said Mr. Jones.
But he never took that dog for a walk.

"That dog is so smelly," said Mrs. Jones. But she never gave that dog a bath.

"That dog is so boring," said Joe and Josephine Jones. But they never played with that dog. All they ever did was argue and fight, argue and fight.

And so **that dog** was sad, sad, sad. He lay on the ground and howled as though the end of the world had come.

Then he stopped. There was no point in crying, oh no.
That dog jumped up.

I'll show them, he thought. *I'll make them take notice!*
That made him feel better, oh yes it did.

So one night, when Mr. Jones and Mrs. Jones and Joe and Josephine Jones were all asleep, **that dog** packed his bag, put on his best scarf, and crept out of the house. Creep, creep, creep.

And he ran away.

He ran away over here.

He ran away
over there.

After a while, he felt hungry.
But there was no one to feed him,
not even mean, moody Mr. Jones.

That dog got hungrier
and hungrier. "I'll have to get
a job," he said.
So he did.

That dog worked hard. Oh, he worked so hard, oh yes! He washed a **million** plates in a restaurant.

He drove a taxi here and there,

there and here.

He swept out
the stables.

Sweep,
sweep,
sweep.

He picked up litter in the park.
Little by little, people began to notice him.

Pick, pick, pick,

That dog was always the first one to help old
ladies across the road. He liked helping people.

So he learned to be a
firefighter and a nurse . . .

. . . and a helicopter
rescue pilot,

RESCUE

a car mechanic,

and a farmer.

That dog never gave up! He even went to the library and read every single book, until he knew everything.
EVEN . . .

how to make new friends.

When the Jones family finally noticed **that dog** on TV they grumbled, "That's our dog!"

But **that dog** didn't need the mean, miserable Jones family anymore, oh no.

Because at the end of a hard day's work, he knew just

where to find the people who loved him the most. Because . . .

THAT DOG was
AMAZING!